## Thanksgiving With Strangers

"Are you really going to help serve dinner at the shelter for homeless people on Thanksgiving?" Suzie asked at recess.

Jessica frowned. "I'm not sure. My parents want us to," she said. "But I don't think I will."

"You shouldn't," Suzie said. "It's a horrible, rotten place."

"How do you know?" Jessica asked.

Suzie turned pink. "Oh, I, um . . . I went there once with my mother to drop off old blankets. I couldn't wait to leave."

"Really?" Jessica said.

"And besides, Thanksgiving is best at your own home, not with strangers you don't know," Suzie continued. "I wouldn't go for anything."

# Bantam Skylark Books in the SWEET VALLEY KIDS series

SWEET VALLEY KIDS

# THE BEST THANKSGIVING EVER

Written by
Molly Mia Stewart

Created by
FRANCINE PASCAL

Illustrated by
Ying-Hwa Hu

A BANTAM SKYLARK BOOK ®
NEW YORK · TORONTO · LONDON · SYDNEY · AUCKLAND

RL 2, 005–008

THE BEST THANKSGIVING EVER
*A Bantam Skylark Book / November 1992*

*Sweet Valley High® and Sweet Valley Kids are
trademarks of Francine Pascal*

*Conceived by Francine Pascal*

*Produced by Daniel Weiss Associates, Inc.
33 West 17th Street
New York, NY 10011*

*Cover art by Susan Tang*

ISBN 0-553-48007-3

*Published simultaneously in the United States and Canada*

PRINTED IN THE UNITED STATES OF AMERICA

CWO     0 9 8 7 6 5 4 3 2 1

# THE BEST
# THANKSGIVING
# EVER

# CHAPTER 1

# Traditions

"I have a baked-bean sandwich for lunch today," Amy Sutton said, peeking into her lunch bag. "What do you have?"

"Tuna fish," Elizabeth Wakefield said.

"Same here," added Elizabeth's twin sister, Jessica.

Lila Fowler opened her milk carton. "You two are always the same."

Elizabeth looked at Jessica and shrugged. "That's the way it is with identical twins," she said with a smile.

Elizabeth and Jessica were the only identical twins in the second grade at Sweet Valley

Elementary School. Both girls had blue eyes and long blond hair with bangs. They didn't usually dress alike, but when they did, even their friends had a hard time telling them apart. The only way to be sure who was who was by checking the name bracelets they wore.

Another way to tell the twins apart was by seeing them play at recess. Elizabeth loved to make up exciting adventures to act out, or to join in a game of soccer. Jessica preferred less messy games such as double-dutch jumprope or going on the swings. Back in class Elizabeth always paid close attention to the teacher. Jessica thought passing notes to her friends was more interesting than multiplication and spelling.

But even though they were different in many ways, Elizabeth and Jessica were best friends. They shared a room, they shared toys, and they shared secrets. Being identical twins was very special to them.

"I wish I could have a baked-bean sandwich every day," Amy said with her mouth full.

"You wouldn't want a baked-bean sandwich for Thanksgiving, would you?" Elizabeth asked. It was the Friday before Thanksgiving.

Amy nodded. "Sure, why not?"

Jessica shook her head. "For Thanksgiving you're supposed to have turkey, stuffing, potatoes, gravy, cranberry sauce, peas, and apple pie," she said firmly. "The Pilgrims didn't have baked beans."

Winston Egbert was listening from across the lunchroom table. "At my house we have rice instead of potatoes," he said. "It's a tradition."

"We have pumpkin pie instead of apple pie," Todd Wilkins added. "And we always have glazed carrots with mini-marshmallows."

3

Elizabeth noticed that Suzie Nichols was listening to the conversation, too. Suzie was in the twins' second-grade class. She also was one of the best dancers in the twins' after-school modern dance class. "What does your family have for Thanksgiving, Suzie?" Elizabeth asked. "Potatoes or rice?"

"My mom always makes wild rice," Suzie answered.

Jessica looked up. "Hey, Suzie, I thought that last year you told us that each person in your family gets to choose one kind of food to have for Thanksgiving dinner."

"I know what I'd choose if we did that at my house," Amy spoke up. She smiled and looked around the table. "Baked beans."

Everyone laughed except for Suzie. "What are you going to ask your mother to make this year?" Jessica asked Suzie.

"Nothing," she answered quietly. "My mom isn't cooking anything special this year."

"That's too bad," Elizabeth said. "One of our favorite traditions isn't happening this year either. Grandma and Grandpa Wakefield always come to our house for dinner, but they're away on a trip. They won't get to eat any of our mom's famous rhubarb pie."

Jessica grinned. "That just means there'll be more pie and turkey and stuffing for us!"

At dinner that night, Mr. and Mrs. Wakefield announced that they had a serious matter to discuss.

"What is it?" asked Steven, the twins' older brother.

"Since Grandma and Grandpa aren't celebrating Thanksgiving with us, we thought we'd do something different this year," Mrs. Wakefield said.

Mr. Wakefield nodded. "Mom and I are going to volunteer to serve Thanksgiving dinner at the shelter for homeless people downtown."

"We'd very much like you kids to help us," Mrs. Wakefield said. "But only if you want to."

"Who lives at the shelter?" Elizabeth asked.

"I know who," Jessica said, frowning. "Creepy people and bums live there."

Mr. Wakefield shook his head. "They aren't creepy, Jessica. They're poor, and some of them are sick. They need us to care about them, especially on holidays."

"That's right," Mrs. Wakefield said. "Not everyone is lucky enough to have a nice house like ours. Some people don't have any place to live at all. The shelter gives them hot meals and a bed to sleep in at night."

"Helping at the shelter would be a kind of sharing, right?" Elizabeth asked.

"Yes, that's very well put," Mrs. Wakefield said, smiling.

"I'll help," Steven said, twirling spaghetti onto his fork. "As long as they have turkey and stuffing."

Mr. Wakefield laughed. "Don't worry, they will. But you won't be able to eat before everyone has a full plate."

Jessica was staring down at her spaghetti. "I don't want to go there," she said. "I want our Thanksgiving to be the same as every other year."

"You don't have to go if you don't want to," Mrs. Wakefield said. "We can leave you with the DeVitos." The DeVitos were the Wakefields' next door neighbors. Jessica loved playing with their baby girl, Jenny. "But helping at the shelter won't interfere with our family celebration," Mrs. Wakefield continued. "The

8

shelter's dinner is in the afternoon. We'll have our own Thanksgiving dinner in the evening."

"If any of you still has an appetite left," Mr. Wakefield said. He looked over at Steven, who was helping himself to a third portion of spaghetti.

Mrs. Wakefield smiled. "Please think about what we've said," she told Jessica. "I'm sure the shelter won't be as grim as you expect it to be."

Jessica nodded. "I'll think about it. But I probably won't change my mind."

# CHAPTER 2

# Dance Class

Monday was the beginning of the school's annual holiday clothing drive. Students in all the grades brought in clothes that were too small for them. Then the school gave the clean clothing to needy families.

"That was my favorite shirt," Jessica said at the end of the day. The bell had rung and she was taking a last look at the clothes she had outgrown. They lay on top of a pile in the back of their classroom.

"Now it can be someone else's favorite shirt," Elizabeth said. She patted the red sweater she had brought in. "I hope my sweater goes to a nice person."

"Who cares? Come on," Lila said from her desk. "Ellen's mother is driving us to the dance studio. We have to go."

Jessica, Elizabeth, Lila, and Ellen Riteman gathered their books and hurried to the door. "Where's Suzie?" Elizabeth asked.

Jessica looked back. Suzie was standing by the pile of used clothes, holding up a jacket.

"Hey, Suzie," Jessica called. "We're going to be late. What are you doing?"

Startled, Suzie dropped the jacket and turned around. Her face was pink. "I wasn't going to take it!" she said quickly.

Lila made a face. "No one said you were. We just want you to hurry."

Suzie followed as the other girls ran outside. Mrs. Riteman's station wagon was waiting by the curb, and the girls all piled in for the short ride to the dance studio.

When they arrived, they waved goodbye to Mrs. Riteman and then hurried inside to get ready for class. "Our parents want us to volunteer at the homeless shelter on Thanksgiving," Jessica told the other girls as they were changing into their leotards.

"Homeless shelter?" Lila exclaimed. "Who would want to do that?"

Elizabeth pulled on her leg warmers. "I do. I think it's good to help people."

"But only poor people stay at shelters," Lila said in her know-it-all way. "Poor people like the ones who are going to get our used clothes."

"So what?" Elizabeth began. "Just because they're poor, it doesn't mean they're not nice people. My mom says—"

"Class is starting," Suzie interrupted. She ran out of the locker room.

Jessica got up and walked out with Lila. "I don't want to go there," she whispered. "I don't want to spend Thanksgiving with a bunch of weird strangers."

She didn't get a chance to say anything more because it was time to warm up. Ms. Garber, their dance teacher, told them to start their arm and leg stretches. Jessica was concentrating on her arm placement when she noticed Suzie talking to Ms. Garber in a corner. They were talking so quietly that Jessica couldn't hear a word they were saying. It made her curious.

"What do you think they're talking about?" she asked Ellen.

"Maybe the recital," Ellen answered. Ms. Garber was planning a dance recital, and everyone was looking forward to being in it.

Lila stretched her arms above her head. "Suzie's probably going to get a solo."

"Do you think so?" Jessica said worriedly. "I hope there's more than one."

As she watched, Ms. Garber gave Suzie a hug. But Suzie didn't look very happy, so Jessica decided that they probably hadn't been discussing the recital after all.

"Now, let's see those arms and legs moving," Ms. Garber said, clapping her hands in rhythm.

Jessica smiled. "You know what I have to be thankful for on Thanksgiving?" she said to

Elizabeth as they did the rest of their warm-up exercises.

"What?" Elizabeth panted.

Jessica caught her breath. "I'll be thankful we don't have dance class every day!"

# CHAPTER 3

# The Phone Mystery

At the end of dance class, Elizabeth changed back into her school clothes and put her leotard and leg warmers into her blue duffel bag. By the time she finished, everyone else had left the locker room.

Elizabeth hurried outside, where she found Jessica talking to Lila and Ellen. "Is Mom here yet?" she asked.

"Nope," Jessica replied. "I hope she gets here soon, though. All that dancing made me hungry."

Ellen giggled. "I know what you mean. If I don't have a snack soon, I'll probably starve to death."

Just then Elizabeth noticed that Suzie was sitting by herself on a bench, apart from the others. She walked over and sat down next to her. "Hi, Suzie," she said. "Want us to give you a ride home?" The Nicholses' apartment wasn't far from the Wakefields' house. Suzie and the twins sometimes shared rides home from dance class, although they hadn't done it lately.

"No!" Suzie said loudly, her eyes wide.

Elizabeth looked at her in surprise.

"I mean, no thanks. My mom's coming," Suzie said. She glanced down the street.

Elizabeth glanced down the street, too. She wondered if something was wrong with Suzie. Lately, Suzie had missed school several times, and she didn't play at the park anymore.

"Suzie," Elizabeth said softly. "Is something wrong?"

18

"No, nothing's wrong," Suzie replied quickly. "Everything's fine." She jumped up. "There's my mom. I've got to go." She ran down the sidewalk toward her mother, who was walking toward them carrying Suzie's younger brother.

"Bye," Elizabeth called after her. She wondered why Suzie's mother was walking instead of driving. It was several miles from the dance studio to the Nicholses' apartment building.

Elizabeth was still thinking about Suzie when she arrived at home. "Mom," she said as she put her duffel bag down in the kitchen. "Can I invite Suzie Nichols over to play after school tomorrow?"

"Good idea," Jessica said, pouring herself a glass of orange juice. "She hasn't come over in about a billion years."

Suzie and the twins used to play together a lot, although they hadn't gotten together for a

few weeks. All three of them loved playing in the woods behind the Wakefields' house, and Elizabeth was eager to show Suzie the fort that she had built there. She also wanted to find out why Suzie had seemed so different lately.

She sat down at the table. "Suzie seems so sad these days. I wonder if something's wrong."

"Suzie Nichols?" Mrs. Wakefield said in surprise. "She's such a cheerful chatterbox."

"Not anymore," Jessica said. "Now she's as quiet as a mouse."

"Well, that is strange," Mrs. Wakefield agreed. "Maybe playing with you will cheer her up. So of course you can invite her over."

"Thanks, Mom. Do you think I could call her instead of waiting until tomorrow?" Elizabeth said.

"Sure." Mrs. Wakefield handed Elizabeth the second-grade class list that was stuck to the refrigerator with magnets. The names and phone numbers of all the students in the twins' class were listed in alphabetical order. Elizabeth found Suzie's name, then dialed the number.

After several rings, Elizabeth heard a click. Then a recorded message came on and said, "We're sorry, but the number you dialed is no longer in service."

Elizabeth hung up the telephone. "Mom? What does it mean if a number is no longer in service?"

"It means that the telephone number doesn't work anymore," Mrs. Wakefield explained. "The Nicholses must have changed their number."

"But how can I call Suzie?" Elizabeth asked.

"I'll call directory assistance," Mrs. Wakefield said. "They can give us the Nicholses' new phone number." But after Mrs. Wakefield spoke to the telephone operator, she just frowned.

"They don't have a new number," Mrs. Wakefield said as she hung up the receiver. "Do you know if the Nicholses moved recently?"

"Suzie's still in our class," Jessica said. "So she couldn't have moved too far away."

Mrs. Wakefield looked puzzled, but then she snapped her fingers. "They must have gotten an unlisted number. I guess you'll just have to ask Suzie in school tomorrow if she can come over the next day."

"OK," Elizabeth agreed.

Her mother's explanation made sense and so did her solution. But Elizabeth couldn't help thinking that this was just one more strange thing about Suzie. She was more determined than ever to find out if something was wrong.

# CHAPTER 4

# Suzie's Secret

Jessica ran out to the playground at recess on Tuesday. "Let's play house," she suggested to Lila and Ellen.

"Let's play castle," Lila said. Lila's father was very wealthy, and the Fowlers lived in one of the largest mansions in Sweet Valley.

Ellen nodded. "Let's definitely play castle! Plain old house is too boring."

"I guess you're right," Jessica agreed. "Besides, I always knew I was meant to be a princess."

"Oh yeah?" Lila said. "Well, if you're a princess, then I'm a queen." She stuck her nose in the air and paraded around, pretending to be a queen.

Ellen giggled and curtsied to both of them. "OK, your majesties. Let's take turns describing our castles. I'll go first. I'm just a duchess, so my castle is small—only two hundred rooms. And I would have servants to do everything for me. One to make my bed, one to do my homework . . ."

"One to change channels on the TV for you," Lila suggested.

"One to eat your vegetables for you!" Jessica exclaimed.

Just then Elizabeth, Amy, and Suzie walked over. "Who's going to eat your vegetables, Jessica?" Elizabeth asked, grinning.

"Oh, hi, you guys," Jessica said. "We're playing castle. We each have to tell about the castle we're going to live in."

"That's right," Lila said. "Mine is going to have two swimming pools—one inside and one outside."

"My castle is going to have three big-screen TVs in every room," Jessica announced.

"I wouldn't want to live in a castle," Amy said. "My dream house would be more like a zoo. I'd have ponies and zebras and seals and lots of other animals."

Elizabeth laughed. "I'd live next door to Amy's zoo, in a tree house like the Swiss Family Robinson's."

"What about you, Suzie?" Ellen asked.

Suzie looked thoughtful. "It wouldn't be fancy. Just a regular house, I guess. And my own room."

"You have to use your imagination," Jessica said. "Otherwise it's no fun. How about having a candy machine in your room? Or having an escalator instead of regular stairs?"

27

Ellen clapped her hands. "An escalator is a great idea! I'll need lots, though, since my castle will be as tall as a skyscraper. You know what else I would have? A princess telephone in every room."

"Oh, that reminds me," Jessica said to Suzie. "We tried to call you yesterday after dance class, but your phone number didn't work."

Suzie didn't say anything.

"Did you get an unlisted number?" Elizabeth asked. "That's what our mother said."

Suzie nodded immediately. "Yes, we got an unlisted phone number, but we're not supposed to tell anyone what it is. It's private."

"That's silly," Lila said. "There's no way *I'd* keep my number a secret. Don't you want your friends to call you?"

Suzie didn't answer. She simply shrugged her shoulders.

"Well, if that's what you want," Lila said in a bored voice. "Who wants to go on the swings with me?"

Ellen followed Lila, while Amy pulled Elizabeth over to the seesaw. Jessica sat down next to Suzie. "Can you come play at our house after school tomorrow? That's what Elizabeth and I wanted to call and ask you."

"I don't know," Suzie said. "I'll ask my mother tonight." She looked around, and then leaned close to Jessica. "Are you really going to the shelter for homeless people on Thanksgiving?"

Jessica frowned. "I'm not sure. My parents want us to, and Elizabeth and Steven said they'd go," she said. "But I don't think I will."

"You shouldn't," Suzie said. "It's a horrible, rotten place."

"How do you know?" Jessica asked.

29

Suzie turned pink. "Oh, I, um . . . I went there once with my mother to drop off old blankets. I couldn't wait to leave."

"Really?" Jessica said. She wished Elizabeth were there to hear Suzie.

"And besides, Thanksgiving is best at your own home, not with strangers you don't know," Suzie continued.

"If you come over tomorrow, maybe we can talk Liz out of wanting to go," Jessica said.

"OK," Suzie said quietly. "I'm going to play on the jungle gym. See you later."

She hurried away.

Jessica wandered over to the swing set and sat down on an empty swing next to Lila. "Have you noticed anything different about Suzie lately?" she asked Lila. "I just asked her to come over after school tomorrow, and she acted kind of weird."

"Suzie's been acting weird a lot lately," Lila replied. "She even fell asleep during spelling this morning. I saw her."

Suddenly Jessica had an idea. "I know! My cousin Kelly acted sad and worried when Uncle Greg and Aunt Laura were thinking about getting a divorce. Maybe that's what's wrong with Suzie, too."

"Try to find out if she goes over to your house," Lila suggested.

Jessica nodded and looked over at Suzie. She loved secrets. And she was beginning to think that Suzie was keeping a big one from everybody.

# CHAPTER 5

# The Shelter

When Elizabeth and Jessica got home from school, their mother announced that she was going to take them shopping for new school clothes.

"The department store is having a sale," Mrs. Wakefield said as they parked downtown. "You two are sprouting so fast it's hard to keep up with you."

Elizabeth laughed. "I'll try not to grow anymore, Mom."

"Me, too," Jessica said, giggling. "But can we get new clothes, anyway?"

Mrs. Wakefield smiled, and the three of

them walked hand-in-hand down the sidewalk. "Before we shop, I want you to see something."

"What is it?" Elizabeth asked, looking up at her mother.

They stopped on the sidewalk in front of a large red building. "This is the Sweet Valley Shelter for homeless people," Mrs. Wakefield said. "I wanted you to see it isn't scary."

Jessica blinked. "It's right here in the middle of town?"

Elizabeth looked at the building. It was like any other building on the street. "There's nothing creepy about it," she said.

"What do you think, Jessica?" Mrs. Wakefield asked. "It's not what you imagined, is it?"

"Well, I guess not," Jessica said uncertainly.

Elizabeth pointed. "Look, there's even an ice-cream store right next door."

A girl and a little boy were standing in front

of the store window. When the girl turned around, Elizabeth saw that it was Suzie. The boy was Suzie's little brother, Tim.

"Hi!" Elizabeth called.

Suzie looked startled to see them. "Hi, what are you doing here?"

"We're going shopping," Jessica said.

"Did you ask your mom if you can come over tomorrow?" Elizabeth said.

"I can't," Suzie said. "She can't pick me up."

"I can bring you home, Suzie," Mrs. Wakefield said.

Suzie shook her head. "But—"

"Please?" Elizabeth asked. "We'll have a lot of fun."

"Tell your mother that I'm perfectly happy to drive you home," Mrs. Wakefield said again. "Actually, I'll tell her myself. Is she buying ice cream?"

34

"She's—" Suzie began.

"She's in there," Tim spoke up. He pointed at the door of the shelter.

Suzie yanked her brother's hand. She looked as though she might begin to cry, but Elizabeth couldn't imagine why.

"Oh, is your mother a volunteer?" Mrs. Wakefield asked.

Suzie nodded hastily. "Yes. Yes, she is. We have to go find her now."

"What's a volunteer?" Tim asked.

Suzie pulled him by the hand. "I'll tell you later," she said as they hurried into the shelter to find Mrs. Nichols.

"I think it's nice that Suzie and her brother come along when Mrs. Nichols volunteers," Mrs. Wakefield said.

"So do I," Elizabeth agreed.

"But she doesn't like it," Jessica said. "You

could tell she didn't want us to know about it."

They began walking toward the department store again.

"There's no reason to be ashamed of helping other people," Mrs. Wakefield said. "It gives you a good feeling."

"Suzie said it was horrible," Jessica insisted. "She told me so at recess."

"It didn't look horrible," Elizabeth said. She looked over her shoulder at the red building. "I wonder why Suzie acted so funny?"

"Because she didn't want to go inside, and neither do I," Jessica said firmly.

Mrs. Wakefield sighed. "OK, Jessica. If you feel so strongly about it, you don't have to help on Thanksgiving Day."

Elizabeth was silent. She just hoped Suzie

wouldn't forget to ask her mother whether she could play at the Wakefields' the next day. She still thought that something was bothering Suzie. And she was more curious than ever about what it was.

# CHAPTER 6

# Playing Dollhouse

"You can sit with me," Jessica said to Suzie as they got on the school bus the following afternoon. Both she and Elizabeth were glad Suzie was coming to their house. "What do you want to play when we get home?"

Suzie shook her head. "It doesn't matter. Whatever you want."

"I built this great fort in the woods behind our house," Elizabeth said. "I thought you might like to see it."

"We'll get dirty," Jessica said. "Let's play inside with our dollhouse. It's a nice big one. Do you have a dollhouse, Suzie?"

"No." Suzie shook her head again.

"Then that's what we'll do," Jessica said, looking at Elizabeth. "OK?"

Elizabeth nodded. "OK. That sounds like fun."

When they arrived home, Jessica, Elizabeth, and Suzie had a quick snack. Then they went upstairs to the twins' bedroom. The dollhouse was in the corner, filled with miniature furniture.

"This is nice," Suzie said. "I wish I could be a tiny doll so I could live in here."

"I think it would be fun to live in an apartment building like yours," Elizabeth told her. "I like riding in elevators."

Suzie bent down to open and shut the front door of the dollhouse. She didn't answer Elizabeth. Then she stood up. "I have to wash my hands," she said, running out of the room toward the bathroom.

Jessica sat in front of the dollhouse and took out one of the miniature tables. Looking at the dollhouse reminded her of seeing the homeless shelter the day before.

"Liz?" she said. "Do you still want to help Mom and Dad on Thanksgiving?"

"Sure," Elizabeth said. "You saw the shelter. It's not spooky or scary or anything like that."

"What about what Suzie told me?" Jessica said. "She said it was horrible there. You can ask her yourself when she comes back."

Elizabeth shrugged. "It doesn't matter. Remember, the Pilgrims didn't have any homes or even any food when they came to America. But the Indians shared with them. That was the first Thanksgiving."

"I know." Jessica knew Elizabeth was right. Sharing was an important part of Thanksgiving. But she still felt nervous about going to the shelter.

Suzie came back into the room, and Jessica nudged Elizabeth with her elbow. "Ask her anyway," she whispered.

"Is the homeless shelter really a horrible place?" Elizabeth asked Suzie. "Jessica says you told her it was."

"Yes," Suzie said in a low voice. "I hate it."

"But what's it like?" Elizabeth wanted to know. "Is it dark and scary inside?"

"Well, people have to sleep on cots," Suzie answered. "There are lots of beds in one big room, and people hang blankets on clotheslines between them to make walls. Every morning the people take down the blankets and put all their clothes and stuff away in bags or suitcases."

"Don't they have any closets or dressers?" Jessica asked, as she looked around her bedroom. She and Elizabeth each had a dresser with five drawers, and they shared a large, walk-in closet.

Suzie shook her head. "No. And it's noisy and crowded. Sometimes babies cry all night, and some of the people are sick and cough a lot so it's hard for people to sleep."

"How do you know so much?" Elizabeth asked. "You must go there a lot with your mother."

"I do," Suzie whispered. "So you see, you wouldn't want to go there on Thanksgiving. It's really awful."

Jessica and Elizabeth stared at each other.

"Can we play with the dollhouse now?" Suzie asked suddenly. "I want to put the oval mirror in the little girl's room."

Jessica nodded. She didn't want to talk about the homeless shelter anymore—now that she was sure Elizabeth was going to change her mind.

# CHAPTER 7

# The Ride Home

Elizabeth, Jessica, and Suzie were re-arranging the dollhouse furniture for the third time when Mrs. Wakefield came into the room.

"Sorry, girls," she said with a smile. "It's six o'clock. Time to take Suzie home."

"You don't have to drive me," Suzie spoke up. "I can walk."

"*Walk?*" Mrs. Wakefield exclaimed. "You're certainly not going to walk home. It's miles from here. I'm driving you and that's that."

"But—" Suzie began.

"We'll all go," Jessica said. "We can pretend

we're princesses again, and Mom can be our chauffeur."

Suzie stood up slowly and followed Elizabeth and Jessica out the door. She hardly said a word as they got into the car and drove toward her apartment building.

Jessica and Elizabeth tried to get Suzie interested in playing princesses, but Suzie wasn't paying much attention. She seemed to be daydreaming.

"Here we are," Mrs. Wakefield said, stopping the car in front of a tall building where Elizabeth and Jessica had visited Suzie several times.

Suzie opened the door and jumped out. "Thank you. I had fun. Bye." She ran to the door of the building and went in.

As Mrs. Wakefield drove away, she shook her head. "I see what you mean about Suzie. She does seem a little bit sad."

Elizabeth turned around and looked out the back window. As she was watching, the door of the apartment building opened, and Suzie walked back out. She headed quickly down the sidewalk.

"Hey! There's Suzie," Elizabeth said, surprised. "She's going somewhere."

"What?" Mrs. Wakefield looked into the rearview mirror, and then stopped the car. "She couldn't have gone to her apartment and come back down so fast."

Elizabeth felt worried. "Maybe her mother asked her to bring something back from the grocery store and she just remembered."

"I don't think Mrs. Nichols would want Suzie to go out all by herself at this time of night," Mrs. Wakefield said.

She turned the car around and began driving back the way Suzie was walking. When she caught up to her, Mrs. Wakefield stopped the car and got out. Elizabeth and Jessica climbed out, too.

"Suzie, where are you going?" Mrs. Wakefield asked. "You shouldn't be walking through the city alone."

Suzie stared up at Mrs. Wakefield with a frightened expression. She looked as though she wanted to run away.

"What's wrong, Suzie?" Jessica asked.

"Aren't you going home?" Elizabeth added, taking Suzie's hand.

For a moment, Suzie didn't say anything. Then she burst into tears.

# CHAPTER 8

# Tears and Fears

"What's wrong, Suzie?" Jessica asked again.

Mrs. Wakefield put her arms around Suzie and gave her a hug. "Now, now. Try to tell me what's wrong. Why aren't you going home to your apartment?"

Suzie sniffled and tried to catch her breath. "We . . . we don't live there anymore," she sobbed.

"Why didn't you say so?" Elizabeth asked. "We can drive you to your new home."

"No!" Suzie choked out, wiping her eyes. "I don't want you to see where I live."

Jessica couldn't believe her ears. "Why not?" she asked.

"Suzie, I can't just leave you here by yourself," Mrs. Wakefield said, stroking Suzie's hair. "You have to tell us where you live. Your parents are probably already worried."

Suzie shook her head and continued to cry while Mrs. Wakefield kept her arms around her. She sounded so miserable that Jessica thought she might begin to cry, too. But finally, Suzie pressed her face against Mrs. Wakefield's side and mumbled something.

"What is it?" Elizabeth asked. "Please tell us."

"Yes, please," Jessica said. "We're your friends."

Suzie looked at Mrs. Wakefield, who gave her a kind nod. "I live at the homeless shelter," Suzie said quietly.

Jessica's eyes widened. "*What?* You live *there?*"

Elizabeth nudged Jessica with her elbow and frowned. "Don't say it like that," she whispered.

Mrs. Wakefield wiped Suzie's face with a tissue. "Do you want to tell us what happened?" she asked tenderly. "How long have you been at the shelter?"

"Only a little while," Suzie said. "We couldn't afford our apartment anymore and there was nowhere else to go."

"But why?" Jessica blurted out. "Don't your mom and dad have any money?"

Suzie's eyes filled with tears again, and she shook her head. "Daddy's last job was almost a year ago and he still can't find another one. We used up all our money."

"But I thought your mother had a job," Mrs. Wakefield said.

"She did," Suzie whispered. "But she quit her job so she could stay home with Tim because daycare cost too much. Then when Daddy lost his job she tried to get hers back, but they'd already hired someone else. So now she takes care of Tim and me while Daddy goes out to look for work."

"He's a housebuilder, isn't he?" Mrs. Wakefield asked. "Not very many people are starting construction projects these days."

Suzie nodded. "That's right. Daddy says lots of people in construction can't find jobs. We might have to move to a different state."

Jessica was so surprised by everything Suzie was telling them that she didn't know what to say.

"I hope you don't have to move, Suzie," Elizabeth said. "We'd miss you if you did."

"How do you get to stay in dance class?" Jessica wanted to know.

"Ms. Garber said not to worry about the money. She doesn't want me to stop dancing, but my father doesn't think it's right not to pay," Suzie said. "I'll have to quit soon."

Jessica thought about how she had worried that Suzie might get the solo in the dance recital. Now she hoped that Suzie *would* get the solo, just so that she would have something nice to look forward to. She couldn't imagine having to move out of their large, comfortable house and into the shelter.

"Come on," Mrs. Wakefield said gently. "Let's go." She took Suzie's hand, and let her sit in the front seat of the car.

Jessica and Elizabeth were both very quiet as they drove downtown toward the homeless shelter. Suzie was quiet, too, except for an occasional sniffle. When Mrs. Wakefield stopped the car in front of the shelter, Suzie got out and walked slowly to the door. Then, she turned around and waved goodbye.

# CHAPTER 9

# Setting the Tables

After the door of the shelter closed behind Suzie, Elizabeth sat back in the car seat and let out a deep sigh.

"No wonder Suzie didn't want us to volunteer on Thanksgiving," Elizabeth said. "She didn't want us to know she lives there."

"I didn't know kids lived in shelters," Jessica said.

Mrs. Wakefield turned around and looked at them both. "How do you feel about volunteering now, Jessica? Does knowing Suzie lives there make a difference to you?"

"If we volunteer, we can eat Thanksgiving

dinner with Suzie," Jessica said. "Maybe that would make her happy."

"That's a nice way to look at it," Mrs. Wakefield said, smiling. "Suzie can sure use some good friends right now."

"Mom?" Elizabeth asked. "Why don't we ask Suzie and her family to live with us? Suzie can stay in our room."

Jessica nodded eagerly. "She can sleep in my bed. I'll sleep on the cot."

Mrs. Wakefield shook her head slowly. "I'm sorry, honey. That might work for a short visit, but our house isn't big enough for two whole families to live in."

"I know," Elizabeth whispered sadly. "But I sure wish it were."

\* \* \*

The next day was Thanksgiving. When Elizabeth woke up, she almost began to put on school clothes, but then she remembered it was a holiday.

"We can wear our new dresses," Jessica said cheerfully, opening the closet. "They're perfect for a holiday. They're so beautiful."

Elizabeth looked at the two blue velvet dresses hanging side by side in the closet. They had bought them the day before, along with some shirts and jeans. Elizabeth wondered how Suzie would feel if she saw them wearing such pretty new clothes, when she had to wear hand-me-downs from the clothing drive.

"Let's wear something plainer," Elizabeth suggested. "That way Suzie won't feel so left out."

"Good idea," Jessica agreed at once. She

pulled out her jeans and a patterned T-shirt. Elizabeth put on jeans and a green T-shirt.

The Wakefield family arrived at the shelter at twelve o'clock. Elizabeth and Jessica looked around for Suzie as soon as they got inside. To Elizabeth's surprise, there were children of all ages there. The younger ones were playing tag, running in and out between the beds at one end of the long room. One older girl was braiding a younger girl's hair, and two men were talking to a woman with a baby.

"It sure is noisy," Jessica said. "Just like Suzie told us."

"But it's not creepy," Elizabeth pointed out.

Suzie walked over and said hello. She seemed surprised to see the twins. "I told you it was terrible here," she said, sounding embarrassed.

"It's not that bad," Elizabeth said. "Can we sit with you for dinner?"

Suzie looked from Elizabeth to Jessica, and back again. "You don't mind that we don't have our own home anymore?"

"No, silly!" Elizabeth said. "We like you just the same as ever."

Suzie smiled.

"Come on, kids," Mr. Wakefield said, coming over to join them. "Everyone has to pitch in and help. Can you smell those turkeys roasting?"

Elizabeth sniffed and nodded. The mouth-watering smell of Thanksgiving turkey made her stomach growl. "I can't wait to eat!" she said.

Soon, the volunteers and the people who lived at the shelter started setting up long tables and draping them with paper tablecloths.

One man was in charge of the salt and pepper shakers and the dishes of cranberry sauce. He passed them out to all the kids to put in place. Mrs. Wakefield carried a tray full of cups of apple juice, and Mr. Wakefield went into the kitchen to help carve the turkeys.

"Who serves the plates?" Elizabeth asked Suzie.

"We have to get in line," Suzie said. "Like at the school cafeteria."

Elizabeth realized that this was going to be a very unusual Thanksgiving. They were going to eat from paper plates instead of Mrs. Wakefield's special holiday china. They would have to wait in line for seconds instead of passing their plates whenever they wanted more. But she knew that didn't matter. What mattered was the spirit of Thanksgiving—the fact that they were all sharing.

Suzie's mother walked over with several baskets full of rolls. "Have you seen your father, Suzie?"

Suzie shook her head with a worried expression. "No. Is he coming back soon?"

"He was supposed to," Mrs. Nichols said. She hurried away to put the rolls on the tables.

"Where did your father go?" Elizabeth asked.

"I don't know." Suzie frowned. "He left right after breakfast. I just hope he comes back in time for Thanksgiving dinner."

# CHAPTER 10

# A Special Thanksgiving

After the hustle and bustle of preparation, it was time for everyone to get in line for dinner. Jessica stood behind Elizabeth and Suzie, and looked around shyly at the other people. She had expected to see scary old bums in the shelter, but everyone looked just like regular people. She smiled at two little boys who were tickling each other near her.

"The food looks good," Jessica said as they were about to be served. She held up her plate for mashed potatoes.

"It does," Suzie agreed. "But it's not like this

every day. That's why I want Dad to get back. I don't want him to miss it."

"I'm sure he'll be here soon," Elizabeth said, trying to sound cheerful.

All three girls filled their plates with food. Then they joined Mrs. Nichols at one of the tables. She was sitting with Suzie's little brother, Tim.

"I saved seats," Mrs. Nichols said, glancing nervously at the door. "One is for your father."

"May we join you?" Mr. Wakefield asked, coming to the table. "Almost everyone has been served, so we can eat together."

Mrs. Nichols nodded. "That would be nice," she said with a smile.

Jessica took a big bite of turkey and then looked around the room. Everywhere she looked, people were sitting down with their full dinner plates. Excited chatter and delicious smells filled the air.

Jessica picked up her plastic fork and knife. This wasn't the traditional Thanksgiving dinner she was used to, but she was enjoying it all the same.

"There are three kinds of pie for dessert," Steven announced cheerfully. "Too bad Mom said I can only have one slice. But tonight I'll have second and third helpings of everything."

"Isn't he a pig?" Jessica whispered to Suzie with a giggle.

Suzie smiled. But she still looked worried. Jessica knew that her friend was hoping Mr. Nichols would arrive soon. Suddenly, Suzie's eyes lit up.

"There's Dad!" she said, pointing to the door.

Everyone turned to watch Mr. Nichols

hurrying toward them. He had a bright, excited smile on his face. "Hello, everyone," he said. "I'm sorry to be so late." He gave Mrs. Nichols a kiss.

"I have good news," he announced. "I found a job today!"

"Congratulations!" Mr. Wakefield said, shaking Mr. Nichols's hand. "That's terrific."

"What kind of job, Dad?" Suzie asked. "Do we have to move far away?"

"There's a large housing development twenty minutes from Sweet Valley that's beginning construction next week," Mr. Nichols explained. "I'll be working there. It'll take at least a year to finish the project, and by that time the construction business should be in better shape. We'll be able to move back to an apartment soon."

Mrs. Nichols threw her arms around Mr. Nichols in a joyful hug.

"Now that's something to be thankful for," Mrs. Wakefield said, smiling from ear to ear.

"Absolutely," Mr. Wakefield agreed. "Let's have a toast."

Everyone raised their paper cups of apple and cranberry juice. "Happy Thanksgiving," Jessica and Elizabeth said at the same time.

"I'm really glad I came to the shelter," Jessica added, looking right at Suzie. "It's *not* a horrible place."

Suzie smiled. "It isn't today."

After Thanksgiving lunch the Wakefields helped to clean up at the shelter. Then they drove home.

"I'm glad we don't have school tomorrow,"

Jessica said from the backseat. "I want to play at the park. Suzie is even going to come."

"It looks as if things are going to work out for the Nicholses," Mr. Wakefield said. He stopped the car at a red light. "Mr. Nichols should be able to find an apartment fairly soon."

"Good," Elizabeth said. "That way Suzie can sleep better at night. She was starting to fall asleep in class."

"And she was absent a lot, too," Jessica added.

"I wish I could miss school whenever I felt tired," Steven spoke up. "I'd play basketball all day."

Mrs. Wakefield laughed. "You'd be too tired to do that. Besides, if you stayed home often enough, you'd get bored very fast."

Elizabeth nodded as the light turned green. "I always think I'm missing something important if I'm absent."

"I miss my friends," Jessica said. "And recess."

She and Elizabeth had nearly perfect attendance records. But that was about to change.

*Will Elizabeth miss something important at school when an accident forces her to stay home? Find out in Sweet Valley Kids #35, ELIZABETH'S BROKEN ARM.*